A NOTE OF MAGIC

MICHAEL KINGSWOOD

 Created with Vellum

CONTENTS

About This Book — v

1. A Note Of Magic — 1

Message From The Author — 43
Mailing List — 45
Supporting Patronage — 47
About The Author — 49
More Books By Michael Kingswood — 51

ABOUT THIS BOOK

Few things in life give Lilly more pleasure than playing her clarinet and making beautiful music.

She never dreamed music might have a magic of its own, or that her band recital might become a battleground between good and evil.

A Note of Magic is a 12,000 word fantasy novelette.

———

Enjoy the book! After you're done, please come to Michael's website and sign up for his mailing list at http://www.michaelkingswood.com/newsletter-signup/. Guaranteed to be spam free, he uses it to announce new releases and special promotions for his fans.

A NOTE OF MAGIC

Lilly wet her lips quickly, then rested them on the mouthpiece of her clarinet and waited. The reed pressed against her tongue, its rough texture and wooden taste familiar and comforting as she readied herself.

All around, the other members of the McClain High School Performance Band—more an orchestra than a band, really—had their gazes locked on a slender woman in a white and yellow sun dress that set off her greying hair, who stood at the center of the semicircle of musicians.

Mrs. Quigley smiled and raised the baton that she carried loosely in her right hand. Then, with a negligible flick of the baton, the band commenced.

It usually did not take very long for Lilly to become caught up in the pleasure of performance, all else forgotten but the notes on the sheet music before her, the imagined ticking of a metronome in her head, and the movement of her fingers along the clarinet's valves as she played her part, and today was no different.

She played, and lost herself in the ecstasy of the moment, not noticing the heat of the bodies all around her—so many that the air conditioning, weak

as it was in this part of the school, could not keep up
—or the sweat that dripped down her back, making
her ruffled blue shirt stick to her skin.

The music was all.

She played, and it seemed as though a force other
than herself sent her fingers over the valves, con-
trolled the quick inhalations and slow exhalations
that created the notes she played.

Henry, the spindly Freshman who sat next to her,
as second Clarinet, reached over to flip the sheet
music over, but she paid him no heed.

Onward, the music carried her, and she began to
feel truly a part of it. It seemed she would float away,
carried on her clarinet's tones to a state of pure bliss,
pure light. For a second, she almost thought she could
see that light, a beautiful pink-white radiance that
bathed over her.

And then that second passed, and with it, the
oneness that she had felt so clearly.

Abruptly, she realized she was no longer in her
seat. She stood, alone amongst all the others in the
band except for the bassists. Hers was the only music
being played, and all eyes were on her.

Her last note turned into a squeak and then ended
abruptly. She lowered her clarinet, her face growing
hot in embarrassment.

"What was that, Lilly?" Mrs. Quigley said, one
eyebrow raised in what normally passed for her stern
expression. But her tone did not convey anger, only
curiosity and...admiration?

Lilly swallowed and tried to grin, but it felt fake.
She glanced around at the other musicians and forced
out a little laugh. "I'm sorry," she said. "I just
got...caught up."

"Please do so again. That was wonderful."

Lilly gaped at Mrs. Quigley's words.

"But," the teacher added, "save the improvisation

for after Mozart, hmm?"

Lilly nodded and hastily sat down, still flushing. She made a point of re-arranging the sheet music on her and Henry's music stand, determinedly not looking anyone else in the eye. How much time was left in this period? She was not sure she could stand to remain there much longer, mortified as she was.

Just then, as if cued by her thoughts, the bell rang.

Half the band stood up and began putting their instruments away. Mrs. Quigley had to rap her own music stand twice with her baton before they gave her their attention.

"We have one more rehearsal on Wednesday, and then the recital on Friday night." Mrs. Quigley beamed a brief smile. "Be ready."

There was a quiet murmur from the gathered students, then, en masse, they packed up and bolted for the door. Such was the danger of scheduling rehearsal for the final period of the day. Most of the upper-classmen had missed free periods—an early departure form school, really—to be there, but that did not mean they wanted to remain even a minute longer than necessary.

Lilly did not hurry, though. Even had she felt up to dealing with their stares, she would not have left with them. She actually liked playing her clarinet. Loved it, really. Oh, she had no doubt the others enjoyed band as well, to some extent or other, but it did not compare with the joy she took from it. That much was obvious. And so she always remained after for a while, practicing on her own.

She raised the clarinet to her lips and inhaled, but Mrs. Quigley's voice broke her concentration. "Did you come up with that solo part during these little extra sessions of yours?"

Lilly looked back at the teacher and found her staring back at her curiously, her hands resting on her hips. She shrugged. "Not sure. I lost track of what I was playing, just then."

Mrs. Quigley watched her in silence for several seconds, and Lilly felt the hair on the back of her neck stand on end. There was something odd about the way the teacher was looking at her. Something almost... She could not put words to it, but all of a sudden she felt extremely wary of Mrs. Quigley.

Then the moment passed and Mrs. Quigley flashed that smile again. "See you Wednesday," she said, then she, too, turned to leave the room. She paused at the door and looked over her shoulder at Lilly. "Practice hard."

The door shut behind her with a barely audible click, leaving Lilly alone with her clarinet, and with the notes.

Twenty minutes later, Lilly stepped out of the front entrance to the school into the bright warmth of the late spring afternoon and looked around. The student parking lot off to the right was mostly empty. Few of the extracurriculars held meetings on Mondays, so there was no reason for most of the upperclassmen to remain after the final bell.

All the same, a few of her fellow Seniors gaggled there, chitchatting and laughing together. Football jocks mostly, from the look of the boys, and cheerleaders. Lilly watched the empty-headed hussies for a minute as they threw themselves at the muscled guys, marveling at how they could be so transparently brazen without catching any hell for it. If she ever thought of behaving that way...

And of course, there was Katrina, the first violin, all long legs and graceful curves, her perfect blonde hair tossing as she laughed at one of the jocks' words, her violin case tucked under her arm. It was simply not fair. She was everything Lilly wished she could be: beautiful, popular, smart, and a brilliant musician.

Their eyes met, and Katrina's smile turned slyly vicious. She gestured Lilly's way, and the group of jocks and hussies looked over in her direction. One of the cheerleaders said something, and the group of them laughed, still staring straight at her.

Lilly made a point of turning left, away from the parking lot and the other students. She lived close enough to walk home; even if she had a car, she would not have had a need to go to the parking lot.

She was not fleeing from their mocking stares. She was *not*.

Or at least that was what she told herself.

She turned the corner of the building, leaving the floozies to their victims, and headed down the edge of the athletic fields toward her street, at the far end of the complex. Off to her left, the baseball team had suited up for practice and was in full swing. Idly, she noted that the cheerleaders did not bother to practice in view of these particular jocks. All the better for them.

She passed the baseball backstop and continued on, her thoughts already leaving the boys and their diversions. A tune passed through her head. She recognized it from earlier, when she had gone off during rehearsal. It had seemed so clear then, but now it echoed through her memory like a dream half-remembered. She knew that tune, somehow. But it vanished as soon as she tried to take hold of it. She should be able to hum it, but somehow it eluded her, the notes flitting out of her mind as soon as they came.

What was...

Something slammed into her and she fell forward onto the turf, letting out a high-pitched yelp that sounded horrid in her own ears. She threw out her hands to catch herself, her book bag flying wide from the effort, but only managed to land jarringly on her left wrist.

Damn, that was all she needed was to hurt herself before the recital.

Something heavy lay atop her, and she had to squirm to get out from beneath it. She rolled over onto her back, working her wrist gingerly and biting her lip, both from the pain and from the effort of holding back a salty curse one of her mother's boyfriends had let loose one time.

A boy rolled the other way—it must have been he who landed atop her—and she scowled. "What do you think you're - "

The words cut off in her mouth as the guy pushed himself up onto his hands and knees and looked at her, concern on his face. She recognized him immediately: Josh Harrington. Her stomach did a little flip in her belly as his bright green eyes met hers and he flushed with embarrassment.

"Sorry, Lilly," he said, getting to his feet in a hurry and offering her a hand up. "Didn't see you there."

She should have snapped back some witty retort, but right then all thought left her as she looked up at him. A few strands of his dirty blond hair hung out dashingly below the brim of his ball cap, and his practice uniform was grass-stained where he had landed on the turf. On *her*. She forced down a little shiver as her mind tried to take that thought another six steps farther than it should have.

"S'ok," she managed to say, and started to her feet. She took his hand, not wanting to refuse the effort at politeness, and a second later almost wished she had not.

A little jolt excitement, almost electricity, seemed to run down her hand and into the rest of her body at his touch, and her legs stopped working for a second. She half-collapsed back to the ground before she caught herself and got back to her feet.

She turned away, so he would not see the flush she felt running through her cheeks, and looked around for her book bag. There it was, off to the left. And, next to it, a baseball.

"Guess I made you miss your catch," she said. He was an outfielder. It was not good for him to miss catches. She hoped he would not get in trouble for that. "Sorry."

Josh laughed softly, bounding past her to scoop up her book bag and his ball, both. He turned back to her, an easy grin on his face as he held her bag out for her. "Not the first time." How many girls had he run into out here? "Are you alright?"

She was about to nod, but right then the alarm on her watch went off. She glanced down, surprised. She did not remember setting the alarm. Then she saw the time.

3:45.

Something...shifted...within her. A force seemed to shove her aside within her own head, and everything went black.

She needed to hurry; she was almost late.

She snatched the bag away from the boy, murmuring something—she had no idea what—and spinning away from him toward the street. She caught a brief flash of confusion, becoming irritation, on his face before he left her field of view, and then she was off.

She covered the remaining distance to the street, and then down the three blocks to the girl's house, at a run.

She burst through the front door and hardly spared a second to glance around the foyer with its gleaming hardwood and sparse, tasteful furnishing before dashing upstairs. She did not announce herself; the mother would not be home from work for some time. She got to the girl's room and kicked the door shut behind herself, dropping her book bag in a heap on the floor. A quick scan showed everything still in place: the double-bed, neatly made with white-lace blankets off in the corner to her left, the writing desk beneath the window at the foot of the bed, the dresser against the wall to her right, and there, against the wall directly ahead, the music stand.

A rush of relief flowed through her; nothing had been disturbed.

More slowly now, she lifted the foot of the mattress up and pulled out a small bundle of paper from its place of concealment. She flipped through it and, spying the familiar lines and notes of the music, smiled in satisfaction. The pages were still intact.

That thought struck her as silly; nothing on this earth could destroy these pages, or render their notes unreadable. But this was not a game that allowed for mistakes; the consequences of an error would be disastrous beyond the understanding of the simple people around her.

She set the sheet music on her music stand, feeling the weight of her burden distinctly, as she always did when she prepared herself. As she assembled the girl's clarinet, she spared a glance at her watch.

3:55. This would not do.

But there was no help for it. She finished her preparations and set the reed to her lips, her eyes focusing on the first note as she gathered her will. She inhaled slowed, through her nose, then set to it.

The notes came easily, carrying through the room on a wave of energy that made the hairs on her arms stand on and. Her skin tingled in a thousand places as the music took her, pulling her onward almost against her will, her fingers flying across the clarinet's valves and her breathing strong and steady as she played. This was the spell that had touched the girl in band rehearsal multiplied a hundredfold, and she reveled in it.

And yet...what had happened in rehearsal gave her pause. That should not have happened; the girl should not have been able to tap into this, not without guidance. How had...?

She brought herself back to the present with a flash of chagrin. Focus. Focus was required now, lest it all go wrong.

The music began building in a crescendo that filled the room until it seemed the walls would burst apart. And then, all at once, another series of notes joined hers, a lilting harmony that matched and lifted her part to a level greater than she could have managed on her own.

And with the expanse of the song, the light from outside—bright and pure on this nearly cloud-free day—faded, dimmed. In the center of the room, and new radiance began to grow. Pink-white, it pulsed in time with the music, beckoning. Weakly at first but quickly growing more intense in time with the growing harmony until it seemed she must go blind from looking at it. And then brighter still it became until it eclipsed all perception, replacing the world she had been in, leaving nothing behind. Nothing but the music.

Her fingers were a blur; she could not remember when she had last taken a breath. But she felt no fatigue, no shortage of breath. The music carried her, nurtured her, lifted her up into the vortex of light. She billowed upward and her heart gave a little jump at the sudden feeling of weightlessness; familiar and expected though it was, the transition always had that effect. Strange, that. She should have been used to it by now.

She reached the end of her part of the music and let the clarinet lower from her lips, but somehow the melody and harmony continued on without her. The strands of the song reinforced themselves, each preventing the other from fading lest the connection be broken.

Drifting in the pristine glow, she pushed aside the body's reaction and allowed herself to bask in the sense of warmth, of belonging. Of power. She closed her eyes for a moment and just...felt.

When she opened them again, she was no longer alone.

A figure floated in the light before her. Its was blurry, obscured as though being seen through a warped piece of glass, but it was humanoid, with strong features framed by long pale hair. Flowing iridescent robes, their color difficult to determine in the surrounding brilliance, hung from its shoulders, giving the figure air of formality.

She inclined her head respectfully in greeting.

The figure did not speak. Rather, words appeared in her mind. "You are overdue."

"I know," she said, voicing her thoughts aloud. "The girl became distracted. I was forced to intervene."

The figure's features twisted in disapproval. "Is she going to be a problem?"

She paused for a moment, considering, then shook her head.

"Very well. Report."

"I am certain I have located the target. I'll only need a short time to complete preparations."

The figure again looked disapproving. "Time grows short. You know the consequences of error."

"I do."

"See that you keep them in mind." The figure paused. When it "spoke" next, it was with greater warmth. "You have been apart from us for a long time. Your presence is missed."

She felt a flush at the change in tone, and could only incline her head again, more deeply.

"Have you anything else?"

She considered mentioning the incident during the girl's music rehearsal this day, but decided against it. It was nothing she could not handle, nothing to worry over. She shook her head.

"Very well. Report again in two days, and be prepared to complete your task quickly." The figure was back to formality and command. "Much depends on your success."

She inclined her head again, in farewell this time.

Then, with a flash of brilliant white, then connection broke and the figure was gone.

"What's going on in here?"

Lilly gave a little start and almost fell off her bed. She blinked her eyes, bringing them into focus, and sat up, confused.

Her bed. What was she doing on her bed? The last thing she could recall was picking herself off the grass where Josh had run into her, the way the sunlight glinted in his eyes... She shook her head, suppressing the thought, and looked over toward her bedroom door, where her mother stood with her hands on her hips, staring at her with a mixture of concern and irritation.

Mother was everything Lilly was not: tall and willowy while Lilly was short and—how did grandmother say?—big boned. Mother's hair was dark, just a shade less than black, and she wore it up, giving her an elegant but businesslike look when matched with the dark pants suit that seemed to both show off her curves and conceal them at the same time. She spent plenty of time at the gym to keep herself looking that way, Lilly knew. But—and Mother would be mortified if she realized Lilly knew this—she also had made use of professional help to do so. That's what Lilly heard one of the girls at school call getting plastic surgery once.

"Are you alright?" Mother asked, concern growing on her face as she took in Lilly's appearance.

"Yeah." But was she? She glanced at the clock hanging on the wall above her desk, and stopped short. 5:45. She had lost two hours this time.

Lilly shivered. Several times over the last weeks, she had found herself sitting someplace, or lying on her bed, unable for account for some amount of time. Sometimes just a minute or two, sometimes more: a half hour or forty-five minutes. It had made her nervous, but she had never lost *this much* time before.

That was downright frightening.

"The front door was standing wide open. I thought someone had..." Mother stopped, shaking her head. "Are you sure you're alright?"

Lilly nodded quickly, not trusting herself to speak just then. Mother already thought her strange. If she knew about the lost time Lilly had experienced lately... Lilly had no desire to be poked and prodded by a bunch of doctors, or worse get taken to a head-shrink. She had just been very tired, and had fallen asleep is all. Nothing more.

Easy to say.

"I'm going to get started on dinner. Come down and help?"

Lilly nodded again, quickly. "Be right there."

Mother smiled then, reassuringly, and turned to

walk back downstairs, leaving Lilly to sit on her bed and try to get her thoughts in order. She was not very successful.

Lilly walked into the band's rehearsal room, feeling strangely anxious. It had been building up within her all day, the feeling that something momentous was about to happen. She tried to shrug it off as nerves over the impending recital, now only two days away, but could not. She had played in many recitals, both solo and in an orchestra, over the years, and before audiences far larger than they expected in the school's auditorium.

No, there was something more that had her worried. She just could not figure out what.

Mrs. Quigley turned from where she stood near her conductor's music stand, baton in hand, and smiled in greeting. As usual, she was dressed conservatively. Also as usual, her smile seemed just a tad wider for Lilly than for the boy carrying a violin case who brushed past her.

"Ready to go?" the teacher said.

Lilly just shrugged and moved to her seat.

Henry was already there, his clarinet fully assembled and the music sitting on their stand. His blond hair was frizzled as usual, his blue t-shirt wrinkled, and he was sucking on his instrument's reed like it was a lollipop.

Gross.

She sat down next to him, smoothing her loose, flowery skirts absently before setting her clarinet case down and opening it up.

Henry pulled the reed out of his mouth and grinned at her. "Excited?"

Lilly pulled the pieces of her clarinet out and

began fitting them together, pausing only to shrug slightly in answer.

He was not to be dissuaded. "I can't wait. Friday is going to be awesome!" He tested the reed with his thumb then nodded and slid it into place on the mouthpiece of his clarinet. "My grandpa's coming to town just for this."

Lilly tried to give him an encouraging smile, but her heart wasn't into it. For whatever reason, his talking about the coming recital set her heart to racing all of a sudden and she felt a flash of something that was not quite fear.

But that didn't make any sense.

She finished assembling her instrument and wetted the reed, then set it into place. She looked around the room quickly.

The rest of her band-mates were all seated. From all around the room came the sounds of various instruments being tuned or run through arpeggios, a chaotic mass of sound that somehow managed to be pleasing, despite its lack of structure.

It was a familiar pattern, oft repeated, and she found herself calmed by it. There was nothing to worry about, nothing at all.

A couple minutes passed, then Mrs. Quigley tapped her baton onto the top of her music stand. It did not make a loud noise, but the rhythm of it cut through the various musicians' preparations easily, and the noise around the room died out.

Mrs. Quigley's eyes moved over the group, assessing. And was Lilly imagining things or did they pause on her longer than on anyone else? Again she felt a shiver of almost fear, but then the feeling passed as the teacher's gaze swept past her.

"Two days to the recital," Mrs. Quigley said. "This is our last rehearsal, so let's make it a good one." She raised her hands, and, in unison with her motion, the band raised their instruments to positions of readiness.

They began.

Almost immediately, the tension that had been filling Lilly seemed to wash away. The notes flowing out of her lungs and through the valves in her clarinet seemed to lift her; she almost felt she was going to float away. Her head swam, and the musical symbols on the pages Henry had placed on the music stand wavered and blurred. Still, she played on. She knew the part by heart, and anyway she could not have stopped herself if she tried.

The song progressed, and she lost herself more and more as the seconds passed. Nothing existed except the next note she was going to play, nothing mattered except the pace of her breathing and the rhythm of her fingers on the valves. Her vision narrowed, the faces of her bandmates fading into a blur all around her.

And then, a light. A glorious white-pink light that warmed her to core of her being.

Unbidden, a different piece of music came into her mind, familiar despite her certainty that she had never played it before. Without thinking about it, she changed the rhythm of her breathing, and her fingers moved to key the new melody.

It came so naturally. It was so...right.

No!

A voice that was not her own seemed to shout in her head, knocking her off her rhythm.

Not now, not yet!

She faltered, shaken to the core, but the call of the music was so strong, the light so welcoming. She could not stop herself...

She felt a...wrenching. Heard an inaudible curse inside her head.

And then everything went black.

Lilly floated in nothingness, for how long she did not know.

Slowly, she came to realize that she existed, that she was, in fact, able to think. But she could not see, could not hear. Could not move. It was like she was a thought without a body, unable to do anything.

A shiver of fear ran through her. What had happened to her? Where was she?

All around, there was only blackness, only silence. She tried to speak, but no sound came out of her mouth.

The fear grew, nearing panic. Her hair felt as though it were standing on end, and her body was damp with cold sweat.

That was something at least. She could feel.

And then she could hear. Slightly. A distant murmuring, like voices speaking softly from across a room. She could not quite understand...

She strained toward the sound, struggling to move.

Finally, after what seemed a year, her head turned, just the slightest bit. And that small motion unlocked the floodgates. First her fingers and toes, then her wrists and ankles began to respond to her commands, and through the blackness, a light began to grow.

Dimly at first, just the faintest of red in the black. But gradually increasing in intensity. And with it, the sounds grew louder as well.

"...don't know how she did it," a voice, sibilant and gentle-sounding, said with more than a hint of confusion.

She turned her head again, and the sounds fell to a murmur once more, before a second voice, deeper and more commanding than the first, became understandable.

"This could ruin everything." The second voice sounded upset.

The redness of the light struck a memory in Lilly's mind: closing her eyes against her mother suddenly flicking on a light switch, to keep the sudden brightness from overwhelming her. The light was just like that, like a lamp shining against her closed eyelids.

She strained, and her eyes opened a crack.

Immediately she knew where she was: her bedroom. She recognized the pattern on the ceiling, where she had once tried to paint a scene when she was little. She was lying on her bed.

But the light that shown around her was not from any lamp. It was white-pink, and warm. Just like the light she had glimpsed in rehearsal earlier. What was going -

She raised her head, and her breath caught in her throat. A nimbus of pink-white floated in the air at the foot of her bed, and within it was a being of some sort. More a silhouette than anything else, but it was a creature, she was sure of it. And sitting next to her, on the bed, was another creature, seemingly made of pure light. She could not make out many details of either being except that they were human-shaped, with long pale hair and clad in translucent clothing, and lovely beyond anything she had ever seen.

The stern voice continued, coming from the being in the air. "You must - "

Lilly's squeak as she finally found her voice cut the being off, and both creatures spun to face her. The intensity of their gazes froze her muscles; she would have shrunk back, sunk through the bed if she could to avoid those eyes. Eyes that glimmered pink-red and seemed to see through to her soul.

"She's awake!" the stern being said. A second later,

it turned its gaze away from Lilly and toward the being next to her on the bed. "How is she awake?"

The being on the bed was visibly shaken, recoiling from the question and from Lilly both as it sprang to its feet. "I don't - "

"Who are you?" Lilly managed to say, through trembling lips. She did not like how squeaky her voice came out. "*What* are you?"

The being who had been with her on the bed gathered itself quickly and moved closer, reaching out an arm toward her. "Lilly, don't be afraid. We - "

Lilly pushed herself away from the being's touch.

"This is unacceptable. Put her back to sleep immediately." That was the being in the air again.

"I think it's a bit late for that, Allona," said the being that had been sitting next to Lilly. It looked back at Allona, floating in the glowing nimbus in obvious displeasure, for a moment. Then, after Allona gave a little nod, it turned back toward Lilly.

"I know this is hard," the being said. It slid back onto the bed and approached her.

Lilly pushed herself backwards so hard that her head hit the wall at the head of her bed. She could not bite back a yelp as pain flared from the contact.

The being edged closer, again reaching out to her. "My name is Selene, Lilly." A pause. "*Selene*."

Selene.

The name froze Lilly in place.

No. No, it couldn't be.

Memories flooded into her, of a time when she was little. Playing with her best friend Katrina in the back yard, their games alternating between duets on violin and clarinet and make-believe adventures with their magical friends. They danced through the flowerbeds, careful not to disturb Mother's gardenias, laughing as they saved the princes from the evil witches that had taken them prisoner. And all the while, they imagined their friends laughing with them. Lilly could not remember the name of Katrina's imaginary friend, but hers was named...

"Selene." Lilly said the name softly, her voice wavering as fear, uncertainty, and wonder all fought within her.

The being—Selene—nodded.

Lilly shook her head. "This isn't real. I hit my head or something, and - "

Selene's hand touched her arm, and a feeling of warmth and certainty, of well-being, spread up from her touch and filled Lilly's entire body. The throbbing in the top of her head, where it had struck the wall, faded away between one breath and the next.

Lilly blinked in confusion, and Selene smiled gently. "Lilly," she said. "We've been together for years. You know better than that."

She shook her head. "It was make-believe."

Behind Selene, Allona made a sound that could have been a snort if it wasn't so dainty. "That's your grown-up mind explaining what the child's mind simply accepted. You two have never been apart."

"I don't understand. I've never seen you before. Where have you - ?"

Selene lifted her finger to her brow, then extended it to Lilly's temple.

The warmth from Selene's touch faded and a shiver went up Lilly's spine and her stomach did a little flip. "In my head?" Saying made the reality strike her, and her blood turned to ice. "You've been *inside* me??" He pulled away and bounded off the bed. She had to get away, and the door to the hallway was so close. Surely she could make it before they could catch her.

"Haven't you wondered why music comes to you as easily as it does?" Allona said, some of the sternness leaving her voice. "Why it makes your very soul sing?"

Lilly froze with her hand hovering halfway to the doorknob. "Everyone likes music."

"But not everyone feels it, or can channel it, as you do." Allona paused meaningfully. "People like you are exceedingly rare. Special. It is our purpose to protect them, guide them. That is why Selene has been with you all this time."

"What do you mean?" She looked back at the two glowing beings, some of the revulsion that caused her to flee fading beneath a growing curiosity.

The pair exchanged a look and Selene slid off the bed onto her feet. "There is a power to music, a magic," she said, approaching Lilly slowly. "You've known this your whole life."

Selene's words resonated within Lilly, touching on a feeling that she had experienced seemingly forever, but could not put into words. She nodded slowly.

"Some people are able to tap that power, to shape it, and with it, the world. These people rise above mere competence into virtuosity. If they were left unguided, the effects on both your world and ours would be potentially severe."

Lilly frowned. "So you just jump into people's heads without asking?"

Selene stopped her approach, now a bit more than an arm's reach from Lilly. A slight smile appeared on her face and she shook her head. "No, never. You agreed, don't you remember? You said you wanted me to be with you forever."

"No. When did I - ?" She started to object, but another memory arose. Practicing in the backyard after Katrina had gone home. Giggling as she imagined Selene telling her a joke. Saying she never wanted Selene to leave her.

And Selene replying that they would always be together, no matter what.

Lilly shook her head in denial. "I was *seven*."

"A child sees and accepts truths an adult often will not," Allona said, her tone growing stern once more.

"Katrina had an imaginary friend too. Does she - ?"

Selene shook her head before Lilly finished the question. "The offer was made, but she refused."

"Ok... So you've been, what, riding around in there, watching everything?"

Selene nodded slowly. "And giving a little nudge here and there, to help you learn to best control your ability."

"I see." Somehow, that didn't seem so bad. Although... Lilly froze as an icy lump formed in her stomach. "And...my lost time."

Selene's gentle smile slipped, and that lump became a chill that swept through Lilly's entire body.

"That was you." Selene didn't respond after a second, and Lilly knew she was right. The chill gave way to growing anger. She lifted her chin and scowled mightily. "That was more than just a little nudge. What did you do?"

Selene glanced back at Allona again. "I was... teaching you."

"Teaching me. *Teaching* me?" The anger was real now, a burning fire within her, and he felt her fists clench unconsciously. "Teaching me what?"

The two beings locked eyes for a long several seconds, and then Allona seemed to slump, as though defeated. She gave a little nod and Selene turned back to Lilly.

"You have to understand, Lilly. Not all of our people act for the good. There are some of us - "

"Fugitives," Allona interjected.

Selene nodded agreement and continued. "Some fugitives who reject our people's teachings and seek their own gain through your magic. Most times, we are able to prevent them from causing mischief before they reach your world, but occasionally..." She seemed to take a deep breath. It was the first time Lilly had seen her or Allona make any movement that resembled breathing at all. "Occasionally, they manage to bridge the gap, and we are forced to act more directly."

Lilly raised her eyebrows at them. What this had to do with her, she could not figure, and it didn't explain them mucking about with her memory.

As though reading her thoughts, Allona said, "These fugitives act as any of us would, with humans. They convince a promising musical talent to accept their help, and then take up residence." Lilly flinched at that turn of phrase, but if Allona noticed—or cared—she gave no sign. "But while we nudge and guide, they wrest control almost completely, and the human becomes little more than a puppet in their grasp."

Lilly shuddered. What Selene and Allona had done to her was bad enough, but that was awful. "So...they become possessed."

Selene nodded briskly. "Yes, that is the term your people have used for it. A possessed person can be forced to do great harm if he is not countered. So when we learn a possession has happened, a nearby talent is trained to counter the fugitive's actions and free the possessed." She smiled again at Lilly.

"You mean me."

Allona nodded at Lilly's words. "We believe a possession has occurred at your school. A former acquaintance of ours has crossed over. Since Selene knows the fugitive's methods, she has been teaching you means to counter her magics and force her back to our world, where she can be taken into custody. It had to be done without your knowledge, and quickly, because we only just located her and her plan is nearing fruition." She frowned. "Normally, the instruction could have been spread out over a longer period of time so you wouldn't notice it, and you would have countered her efforts and been none the wiser. But," an accusing look in Selene's direction accented her words, "we were sloppy."

This wasn't helping Lilly be less angry. "You could have just asked. You're no better than your fugitives if you just take over."

Both creatures lowered their eyes.

Selene said, softly, "I'm sorry."

"There was a good reason to not tell you," Allona said, not sounding nearly as contrite as Selene had.

Another lengthy pause. Lilly pressed her fists to her hips and tapped her foot no the floor. "I'm waiting."

Allona gave a little shrug. "In the past, we actively enlisted the aid of talents. They knew of our presence, and we formed powerful partnerships. You've heard tales of seers, prophets, divinely inspired bards, have you not?"

Who hadn't? Lilly nodded.

"Have you ever wondered at their lack in recent centuries?"

"Not really. They were just stories."

Selene chuckled softly. "I think you know better than that, now."

True enough. "Ok. Why haven't there been any prophets lately?"

Allona replied, "Because of Mozart."

That caught Lilly off guard. She blinked in surprise and her mouth dropped open of its own accord. "Mozart. What do you mean?"

"You've heard of the rivalry between him and Salieri?"

"Yeah. It was made up, a story that guy invented to make his play more interesting. And then they made the play into a movie and everyone thinks Salieri was this bad person, when he wasn't at all." And oh, had that made Lilly angry when she learned the truth of it.

"That is mostly true. Salieri had no reason to feel threatened by Mozart at all. He was far more successful than the young upstart from Salzberg, *the* name when it came to opera in Vienna. But," Allona leaned forward, "there is a hint of truth to the tale, all the same. Can you guess what it was?"

Lilly frowned, pondering. Where was Allona going with this? If there was no real rivalry between them, what... Her eyes widened. "Mozart was possessed?"

Allona shook her head. "The opposite, actually. When his guide told him of Salieri's affliction, he worked himself to the bone to learn how to counter the fugitive's designs. But even after he succeeded in helping us capture the fugitive, he began to see signs of possession in others, despite his guide's assurances that it was not so. He pushed himself harder and harder, working to counter a threat that was not really there. And so he died young." She made a loud sigh. "Far too young, and both of our worlds lost out on the music and the magic that he would have created, had he lived."

Allona lowered her eyes again, going silent.

After a couple seconds, Selene said, "That was not the first time a talent was lost early, but his loss was the most poignant. After that, we decided it would be best for the talents to not know of us after they reached a certain age. For their own protection, and ours as well."

The anger had faded, replaced by a lingering resentment, but Lilly found it hard to maintain even that. It made sense, in a weird sort of way. But that left a big question to answer.

"Well, *I* know about you. Now what happens?" Lilly had a sinking suspicion she knew where this was going, but maybe, just maybe, she was wrong.

Selene looked back at Allona, who had recovered her composure. They stared at each other for a time, and Lilly had the feeling they were somehow communicating, even though neither spoke. Finally, Allona gave a shake of her head that, on a human woman, would have been rueful.

"There is no time to train another," Allona said. "It is no longer our way, but there is no choice. If the fugitive is allowed to succeed in her plans, the damage to our worlds, and to the possessed, would be too great." Her glowing eyes turned to look squarely into Lilly's. "Will you help us?"

That's what she thought Allona was going to say. "How?"

Selene spoke up. "You already know what you have to do. At your recital on Friday, a moment will come when the fugitive will attempt a spell. When that happens, just play the music I taught you."

"That's it?"

Selene nodded. "That's it. You already know the song; you've been bursting at the seams with it all week." She smiled apologetically. "That's why I had to take over today. If you had played the song fully, she would have learned how I mean to counter her, and alter her spell to avoid it."

Another shiver went up Lilly's spine. If the showdown was going to take place during the recital, and playing that song in rehearsal could reveal it, that could only mean one thing. "You're saying the fugitive has taken possession of someone in the band."

Selene shook her head. "No. I thought so at first, but now I am certain that the fugitive is taking refuge within your instructor."

"Mrs Quigley?"

Selene nodded gravely. "So. Will you help us, to save your teacher, and both our worlds?"

It didn't seem to Lilly there was much of a choice to make, putting it that way.

Mother gave Lilly a hug. Right there in front of everyone. Flushing with embarrassment, Lilly tried to squirm out, but Mother just tsk'd. She finished the hug with a quick squeeze then stepped back, grasping Lilly's shoulders lightly.

"Have fun tonight, kiddo," she said, here eyes glittering happily as she put on an encouraging. "Knock 'em dead."

Lilly returned the smile with more trepidation than she normally would have felt. Then Mother released her and turned away.

They stood just inside the entrance to the main auditorium in her High School. Other students, parents, teachers, and relations of all sorts mingled about, finding seats and chatting amongst themselves as they prepared for the recital. Most were dressed up, the men and boys in jackets and ties, the women and girls in dresses that were almost, but not quite, to black tie standards.

For her part, Lilly had on a simple dark blue dress with an off-white sash about the waist. She, or really Mother, had put her hair up in a bun at the back of her head that made her forehead feel as though it were being stretched halfway over her skull. But, she had to admit the results looked nice. She almost felt pretty.

Mother selected a row halfway down the room toward the stage. She turned back and waved quickly, then blew a kiss!

Lilly rolled her eyes and, clutching her clarinet case in both hands, turned toward the door. She paused to let an older couple—someone's grandparents probably—enter, then slipped out into the hallway with its endless rows of lockers between classroom doors.

She turned left toward the backstage entrance at the end of the hall, and found herself bumping into a boy. He staggered backwards, and Lilly realized it was Josh Harrington again. Like everyone else tonight, he was dressed up in a jacket and tie. The blue of the jacket went well with his eyes.

Her cheeks flushed red as he grinned at her. "Hey Lilly. Getting a little payback for the other day?"

"No, I... Uh... Sorry." She stumbled over the words, realizing she was sounding like an idiot.

He laughed good-naturedly and grinned a bit wider. "I'm just kidding." He stepped around her and toward the doorway to the auditorium, but paused before he went inside to look back at her. "Good luck tonight. You look great." He winked quickly, and then he was gone, leaving her to blush even brighter.

You should try actually talking with him.

Over the last day and a half, Selene had been popping those sorts of suggestions into her head seemingly at random. Apparently now that her secret was out, she felt free to do so, and it was becoming annoying.

"Shut up," Lilly whispered, and heard Selene's amused laughter in her head.

She put Josh out of her mind and hurried toward the backstage door. The show would be starting soon, and she still had a lot to do to be ready.

Everyone else was already in their places when Lilly stepped out onto the stage. The various musicians were tuning up and there was a feeling of anticipation in the air, stronger than Lilly could recall from any other recital she had played. Looking out at her bandmates, she had to swallow a growing lump in her throat.

She was letting her nerves get the better of her. She never did that.

But then, she had never faced a performance quite like this, had she?

Lilly forced herself to move, sliding past the oboes to reach her seat next to Henry. For once, his hair was under control, and he actually looked halfway put together in a grey suit jacket and red tie. He grinned at her as she got settled in place and started babbling something cheerful, but she didn't hear him as movement from stage right drew her eye.

Mrs. Quigley walked onto the stage, dressed in a clingy off-white evening gown that made her seem to glow in the bright stage lights that shone down on them all.

Or was it more than that? Was the being that had taken possession of her beginning to show itself?

It doesn't work that way, Selene said silently. *She will not reveal herself openly. That would ruin her plans. No one but you will ever know she was involved. If they do notice anything, they'll think it a fancy light show, nothing more.*

That was little comfort. Looking at her teacher— her opponent—she began to shiver. Their eyes met for a second and Mrs. Quigley smiled at her. Lilly felt a surge of adrenalin, and had to stop herself from bolting.

Easy.

She knows. She had to know. About Lilly, Selene

and Allona, everything.

Doubtful. She suspects, nothing more. Be calm, and wait until I tell you. It will be alright.

Easy for her to say.

Lilly went through her preparations mechanically, assembling her clarinet and wetting the reed, then going through some warmup scales the way she always did. Usually, that calmed her nerves before a performance.

Not tonight.

She took a deep breath and forced her eyes away from Mrs. Quigley. She looked around the rest of her bandmates, and for a moment, her gaze came to rest on Katrina, wearing a very pretty pink dress and looking gorgeous as always, who was running through some scales of her own from the looks of things. Their eyes met, and Katrina looked away quickly, her lips drawing down into a little scowl of distaste.

Lilly felt an ache in her chest. Recalling those memories of the two of them when they were little, times she hadn't thought of in quite a while, added an extra twinge to the normal hurt of being snubbed. They had been so close once, but something changed around middle school. Katrina suddenly became the popular one. And then it was as though being friends with her was no longer convenient.

Lilly felt her eyes beginning to water as she remembered the early pain of that lost friendship. Over time, she had set that aside, but...

It hurt all over again, thinking about it.

She looked down at her clarinet, where it rested on her lap, and ran her fingers along it. Her only true friend. That, and Selene apparently, and she wasn't even real.

I'm as real as you are.

Not the same thing.

The silence in her head after that spoke volumes.

Mrs. Quigley stepped up onto her conductor's stand and said some words of encouragement, but Lilly paid them no heed. She was too miserable to care right then, and even if she weren't, it wasn't like she could believe anything the possessed woman said.

And then, the curtain opened.

For most of the first piece, Lilly lagged a half-count behind and missed notes and runs that she normally could have played in her sleep. She just couldn't get into it between her renewed heartache and the anxiety, bordering on outright fear, that she had been fighting all night.

When the song finally ended, and the audience, mostly hidden beyond the glare of the spotlights that shone from the back of the auditorium, applauded, she had a powerful urge to get up and run off the stage.

She couldn't do this. She wasn't good enough, pretty enough, smart enough. Her hair was bad, she was too chubby, she was sweating up a storm from the heat of the stage lights. She was scared. Miserable.

And she was quite sure the being within Mrs. Quigley knew it. She had lost before the fight even began.

No. Lilly. That's not true. You are wonderful, more special than you know.

Selene's feeble attempt at encouragement didn't help at all. She almost got up right then.

"Lilly, are you alright?" Concern shown through in Henry's voice. She glanced aside at him and saw the same in his eyes.

She shook her head, but had no words.

"Hey, it's ok. This is for fun, right?" He smiled that goofy grin and nudged her with his elbow.

Something about the way he said it, the playfulness of the nudge, brought up a half-bitter, half-desperate little laugh from within her.

"Come on, we got this."

She met his eyes, and all that silly enthusiasm that had annoyed her about him before felt right then like a buoy in the middle of the ocean: something to cling to to avoid sinking, She managed a little smile and wiped her eyes with the back of her free hand.

Right then, she could have kissed the goofy kid.

Mrs. Quigley raised her arms and the rest of the band brought their instruments up. Lilly sniffed back the tears that had started to run and lifted her clarinet again.

The second piece was Mozart. The same piece that she had gotten carried away in before. He had always been her favorite, and now, knowing that they had a shared experience, it felt as she began playing that she was playing with him. That he was there alongside her, giving her a little extra helping hand from across the centuries and the gulf between Earth and heaven.

Or maybe that was just some of Henry's enthusiasm rubbing off, or a subconscious boost from Selene.

Or all of the above.

Whatever it was, she felt herself drawn into the performance, finally. The notes flowed out of her, joining with Henry's perfectly as they played their part in the majesty of the whole. Losing herself in the music, her spirit began to soar and the earlier doubts began to slip away. This is what she was made for. The music.

And the magic.

Unbidden, she felt herself moving into the strangely familiar melody that she had begun the other day, the music that she now knew Selene had taught her over these many weeks.

No, not yet. We have to wait until she makes her move.

Her guide's voice in her head snapped her back to

the moment and she faltered over the notes. She had to search on the sheet music for her place, and noticed Henry looking at her from the corner of his eye, his expression questioning and, again, concerned even as he continued to play.

She gave a little shrug and picked up the piece again. But as she played this time, she remained careful to stay in control, to not get too carried away.

And then, just like that, the piece was finished.

Again, the audience applauded. And again, Henry grinned at her and gave her a little nudge.

She grinned back at him, more genuinely this time.

Mrs. Quigley turned to address the crowd, and from stage left some of the backstage crew rolled a stand-up piano and player's bench out onto the stage. With a broad smile, the teacher walked over to it and settled down onto the bench. Katrina, as first violin, stood and moved to Mrs. Quigley's former position at the conductor's stand.

This is it. When she plays, the dark spell will begin.

So when do I...

You will know.

Ok. Here goes nothing.

Mrs. Quigley looked over her shoulder at Katrina and gave a little nod. And for just a second as she turned back to the piano, Mrs. Quigley's eyes met Lilly's. They flashed red.

Lilly's heart skipped a beat. It was real. Part of her had been doubting, despite everything she had seen and heard to this point. But it was real, there could be no denying it now. And knowing that, true fear ran through her.

Katrina turned to the rest of the band and raised her bow like a conductor's baton.

The rest of the band began, but Lilly remained

rooted to the spot for three full beats before she was finally able to make herself play.

The piece was more modern than the rest of their repertoire, by Yanni. At first, Lilly had been leery about it, but after Mrs. Quigley had showed them a video of him playing it at the Acropolis with the London Philharmonic Orchestra, she was sold. The piano and orchestra parts blended together seamlessly, gently, and powerfully.

Lilly would never have thought that one of her teachers would introduce her to a new favorite modern musician, but Mrs. Quigley had done just that.

And now, she was going to use that man's lovely song to poison the well of magic in Lilly's world.

Not gonna happen.

She played, putting her whole heart and soul into it, watching Mrs. Quigley for the cue to slip into Selene's counter spell. Or whatever the right term was.

And then, toward the end of the solo interlude for the piano, the teacher's eyes flashed red again, and it seemed darkness began to swirl around her.

Lilly took a deep breath and began Selene's melody.

Right at that moment, Mrs. Quigley looked over at her, and a malicious grin, a grin of triumph, appeared on her face.

And then the teacher gave a little jerk and the red glow in her eyes went out. She slumped, her fingers stumbling over the piano keys, and shook her head, clearly confused.

For a second, everything stopped.

Lilly lowered her clarinet, confused. Had she just won? That seemed too easy.

A lone violin began to play.

All eyes turned to Katrina, at the conductor's stand. She had the violin solo part, which followed the piano's. She must have decided to start early, to cover for Mrs. Quigley's stumble.

But as she was turning to face the audience, she flashed Lilly that same, maliciously triumphant grin, and her eyes glowed red.

What? No, this can't be right.

There was actual fear in Selene's voice. Almost panic.

What's going on? It was supposed to be Mrs. Quigley.

It was her. The fugitive always claims a host, and sticks with it. Always! There is never a second. Never!

Well it looked like there was a second now. Ok, well if that's how it was going to be, Lilly could take on Katrina easily enough. She drew a breath and lifted her clarinet back to her lips, to play Selene's tune.

You don't understand! It won't work!

Lilly's blood went to ice. What did she mean, it wouldn't work?

I crafted the counter-melody to match the piano part, not the violin. Oh heavens above...

Katrina's solo started out just as the violin solo in Yanni's piece always did, but after a few bars it deviated. The audience, and the rest of the band, would think it an improvisation. But as she played, the darkness that had been gathering around Mrs. Quigley for that brief moment began to coalesce around her.

The dark spell had begun.

What do I do? Lilly shouted the question at Selene inside her head. What do I play?

I don't know I don't know I don't know.

Panic had given way to despair. To defeat. It flowed from Selene into Lilly so strongly that she dropped her clarinet. It bounced off her knees and fell to the floor at her feet.

Oh, all is lost!

Selene's cry became a wail that stretched on an on, drowning out everything else. Lilly's vision swam and she became light-headed as her guide's hopelessness crashed over her. It was a struggle to focus on anything around her.

Damn it, shut up!

The fury that she sent the thought with surprised her; she almost never raised her voice. But it seemed to have done the trick. Selene was quiet.

Lilly shook her head to regain her equilibrium, and Katrina's solo came back full-focus in her consciousness. It was brilliant. Katrina had always been a whiz on the violin, but this... Lilly had never heard her play anything like this. She listened in rapt attention for a few bars, amazed.

And terrified, for as the solo progressed, the darkness grow, becoming a sphere of deepest black hovering a few feet over Katrina's head. All light in the auditorium seemed to be leeching away, even the brilliant spotlights seemed to fade out like the colors in an old photograph: still there, but shadows of their former selves.

Lilly had no idea what that spell would do once released, but it had to be something awful. And she could do nothing but watch it happen.

For a moment, she felt like wailing the way Selene had been.

Then Katrina's playing shifted in tone, and the solo began to seem...familiar, somehow.

It was almost like...

Another memory rose to the surface, from the days when she and Karina used to play duets together in the backyard. There was one simple duet for clarinet and violin...was it...yes, it was Mozart. And was she imagining it, or was that run Katrina just played lifted straight out of it?

Another three bars confirmed it. She was playing

a variation on that Mozart piece.

Lilly knew what she had to do.

She bent over and grabbed her clarinet off the floor. If there's something you need to do to make this work, she thought at Selene, get ready to do it.

Confusion wafted back. *What are you going to do?*

Just get ready.

She lifted the mouthpiece to her lips and paused. It had been years since she last played that piece, but right then it was like she was reading the sheet music, she could see the clarinet part so vividly.

Maybe Mozart himself *was* helping, after all.

She licked her lips, then placed them around her mouthpiece and began to play.

Katrina whipped around as Lilly's notes joined hers in counterpoint, her fingers still flying over the strings even as her brows rose in surprise. Her eyes, glowing brightly red still, narrowed, and her lips compressed into a scowl.

Her other bandmates' eyes turned toward Lilly as well, one and all registering confusion.

"What are you doing?" Henry asked, from his seat next to her.

She paid them no heed. There would be time for explanations later. Assuming there *was* a later. Now she had to focus completely on the music.

From the start, she was playing catch-up. Katrina had the lead, and she was deviating from the baseline of Mozart's original in unexpected ways, and constantly. Lilly had to shift with her, but with no guide, no inkling of where she was going next, their two parts were disjointed, almost dissonant.

It wasn't working. They both knew it, and that smile began to reappear on Katrina's face.

Beads of sweat ran down the sides of Lilly's face, and doubts rose up within her all over again. It wasn't working!

Yes, I have it!

Selene's words filled Lilly with warmth, and suddenly, she felt sure she knew what Katrina's next note was going to be, and what she should do to match it.

Her clarinet line steadied out, becoming more in synch with Katrina's violin, and Lilly felt herself relaxing into the flow of the music more. Her spirits lifted, and she felt buoyed once again. Nothing existed but the music, nothing mattered but remaining in synch with her erstwhile friend, harmonizing with her.

And slowly, as she lost herself more and more, another light began to illumine the stage. Pink-white, like the nimbus Allona had stood within, it shown from everywhere and from nowhere, pulsing in rhythm with Lilly's harmony line.

Katrina noticed the new light as well, and her nostrils flared, the scowl returning, becoming more a snarl. She bore down on her bow, powering the notes from her violin's strings as her fingers flew all the faster.

Lilly pressed hard, taking her breaths quickly when she could and blowing harder to match Katrina's crescendo. But she could not keep the pace up for long. Already she was starting to become light-headed. She was going to have to take a real breath soon.

The light grew brighter, washing out everything except for Lilly, Katrina, and the sphere of blackness in the air.

Still they played on. Lilly's head swam, her lungs burned from the exertion of blowing so hard, for so long. Several strand of horsehair had broken on Katrina's bow. They flapped around with every bow stroke, waving like pendants from her bow hand.

And all the while, the light grew more intense.

It was almost painful to look at now. Lilly had to

squint to avoid being overwhelmed by it.

She wasn't sure how much longer she could continue.

Everything became a wash of pink-white. She couldn't see a thing, except for those glowing red eyes.

And then, all at once, it all vanished. The glow, the black sphere, everything went away, with a POP that echoed silently through Lilly's brain.

Katrina swayed on her feet, the glow lost from her eyes. She stopped playing and looked around with wide, un-focused eyes.

"What?" she said, bringing her bow-hand up to her brow.

And then she collapsed.

Lilly stood up, her clarinet falling from her hands as a great gasp issued from the lips of everyone in the audience and the band both.

Mrs. Quigley shot up from the piano bench and rushed to the conductor's stand, where Katrina lay in a heap. Lilly pushed past the other woodwinds in front of her and moved to the teacher's side.

Mrs Quigley bent over Katrina. She checked her pulse, then glanced out at the audience. "Call 911," she said.

Oh no.

Several members of the audience had cell phones out. Someone was calling Katrina's name, and people were rushing forward. Her parents.

Please let her be ok.

Lilly knelt down next to Mrs. Quigley, who had taken hold of Katrina's shoulders, giving them a gentle shake. "Katrina," the teacher said softly. "Katrina, can you hear me?"

Katrina's eyes fluttered and she took a deep breath. Then she opened her eyes fully. Her gaze locked onto Lilly's for a long second.

"Oh." She blinked. "Lilly. Hi."

Katrina smiled, genuine warmth in that expression for the first time in a long while. And then she passed out again.

By the time the paramedics arrived, Katrina was awake again, and sitting up. She leaned heavily against the conductor's stand and sipped at a cup of water that someone had brought to her.

Lilly sat on her heels and watched in a daze as the medics checked her over, then maneuvered her gently into a wheelchair and pushed her out of the auditorium, her anxious parents following along after them.

It all seemed unreal, like some sort of waking dream. Everyone's voices were muffled, the milling masses a blur aside from her old friend. Even after she had gone, Lilly could focus on nothing aside from concern for her.

She'll be fine. Selene's voice carried calm certainty as she spoke within Lilly's head. *The casting requires a lot of energy, and she used more to fight against the fugitive. But after she's rested it will be as though this never happened.*

That was something, at least, and Lilly felt a weight lift.

You were wonderful. I never...

Selene trailed off, but Lilly had a feeling she knew what the guide was going to say. She never thought it would be as difficult as it had been.

That made two of them.

Lilly drew a deep breath and forced herself to her feet. She swayed for a moment after she stood up, feeling a wave of fatigue wash over her. Right then, she wanted nothing more than to lie down for a week.

She turned to make her way back to her seat, but a hand on her shoulder stopped her.

"Lilly."

She looked back into Mrs. Quigley's eyes. The teacher looked unsettled, confused. And irritated.

"What was that?"

Lilly shrugged slightly. "We always played together," she heard herself say, in a small, distant voice.

Mrs. Quigley's brows furrowed. "I wish you would have told me you two had that cooked up." She stopped and drew a breath, then shook her head. "Next time - "

A man's voice interrupted her, and Mrs. Quigley looked to the foot of the stage, where the Principal stood. He beckoned her over, and Mrs. Quigley released Lilly's shoulder and went to him.

Lilly turned away and slipped past a trio of her bandmates, who were looking at her with strange expressions on their faces. She reached her seat and disassembled her clarinet. By the time Mrs. Quigley announced that the rest of the recital had been cancelled, Lilly had already left the stage.

Mother met her outside the school's main entrance, and greeted her with a big hug. Lilly returned it in kind. They stood there for several moments, and gradually, the daze that had filled Lilly's head receded and the full import of everything that had happened struck her.

Unbidden, tears began running from her eyes.

Mother pushed back and looked at her, concern on her face. "What's wrong?"

Lilly shook her head, unable to put it into words. The fear, the wonder, the despair, the loneliness that she had worked through that night was too much.

She should be feeling triumphant, joyous at their victory. But she didn't. And she didn't know why.

Mother pursed her lips and put an arm around Lilly's shoulder. "Come on, let's go home."

She began to lead her toward the parking lot, where their car was parked.

From behind them came a chorus of male laughter. A group of three boys walked past, and Lilly shrank away as she recognized Josh among them. He stopped what he was saying to his two friends as he saw her and Mother, and paused, gesturing for them to continue on without him.

"Hey," he said, grinning as always. "That was awesome."

Lilly blinked, surprised.

"Never heard anyone play like that. How long had you been working on it?"

Mother gave Lilly a squeeze. "All her life," she said.

"It shows." He gave the two of them a nod. "Well, I'd better not keep Brad and Tommy waiting. See you around." He turned to leave.

Lilly recalled what Selene had said before the recital. Maybe some other time, when she wasn't feeling so ragged, she would not have done it. But right then, she couldn't find it in herself to be afraid any more.

She called out after him. "Where are you guys going?"

Josh stopped and looked back over his shoulder at her. "There's a party over at Scott McClendon's house later." He paused. "Why, do you want to go?"

A big part of her wanted nothing more than to just go home. She almost said no. She meant to say no. But instead, she nodded affirmative.

Maybe being alone, again, like always, wasn't the right answer. At least, not tonight.

He grinned again. "Great. Swing by your place in about a half hour?"

"Ok."

He walked away, and Mother gave Lilly a strange look. Then she smiled gently and led Lilly to the car.

Much later that night, Lilly returned to her bedroom and got ready for bed.

The party had been a revelation, in more ways than one. People were surprised to see her. The performance was on everyone's lips, and she received more compliments than she ever thought to.

But more than that, so many people told her they were glad she had come, and were sorry she hadn't come out with them sooner, that it left her stunned. She had always assumed that she wasn't welcome.

Why would you ever have assumed that?

Selene had not spoken since immediately after the recital. Lilly paused in pulling on her nightgown and considered the question.

It just seemed a given that she wasn't wanted there. It's not like she had ever actually been invited before. People had given her the cold shoulder, by and large.

Uncertainty can make us see things not as they are, but as we fear them to be. You were unsure of them, and they were unsure of you.

Maybe so. Certainly no one had snubbed her tonight, so maybe all it really needed was for one side or the other to make a welcoming gesture.

A little courage can go a long way. I'm proud of you, Lilly.

She smiled as she laid down to sleep.

In her dreams, she played her clarinet with Mozart, and he wore a big smile on his face.

MAILING LIST

If you enjoyed this book and would like word on new releases and special deals from Michael Kingswood, sign up for his newsletter on his website. Guaranteed to be spam-free, you can opt out at any time. And you can rest assured he will not share your information with anyone, for any reason.

https://michaelkingswood.com/newsletter-signup/

SUPPORTING PATRONAGE

47

Michael would like to invite you to become a supporting member of his website. Similar in concept to Patreon, a few dollars a month will give you access to exclusive content, and help him to focus more of his time to writing fun and exciting stories for your enjoyment.

Sign up at his website:

https://www.michaelkingswood.com/membership/
supporting-patronage/

ABOUT THE AUTHOR

Michael Kingswood is 20-year veteran of the US Navy submarine force and a lifelong fan of science fiction and fantasy literature. His work has appeared in numerous collections and anthologies, to include the Fiction River Anthology series from WMG publishing. He holds a bachelors degree in Mechanical Engineering as well as a Master of Engineering Management and a Master of Business Administration. He has four children and currently resides in San Diego.

Find Michael Kingswood online at:

www.michaelkingswood.com

www.facebook.com/michael.kingswood

steemit.com/@michaelkingswood

Or on his Bitchute and Youtube Channels - Story Time With Michael Kingswood

MORE BOOKS BY MICHAEL KINGSWOOD

GLIMMER VALE CHRONICLES

Glimmer Vale

Out-Dweller

Tollard's Peak

Robbed Blind

Wedding Gifts: A Glimmer Vale Chronicles Story

The Falconer's Stairs

Glimmer Vale Omnibus Edition #1

THE PERICLES CONSPIRACY

Passing In The Night

The Pericles Conspiracy

DAWN OF ENLIGHTENMENT

Masters Of The Sun

NOVELLAS

What Lurks Between

The Necromancer's Lair

The Champion

Veritas Morte

STORY COLLECTIONS

Tales Of Adventure #1

Tales Of Adventure #2

Short Story 10-Pack

A Jar Of Mixed Treats

SHORT FICTION

Michael has also published a number of shorter works, links
to which can be found on his website.

www.ingramcontent.com/pod-product-compliance
Lightning Source LLC
Chambersburg PA
CBHW032052180726
48284CB00004B/1302